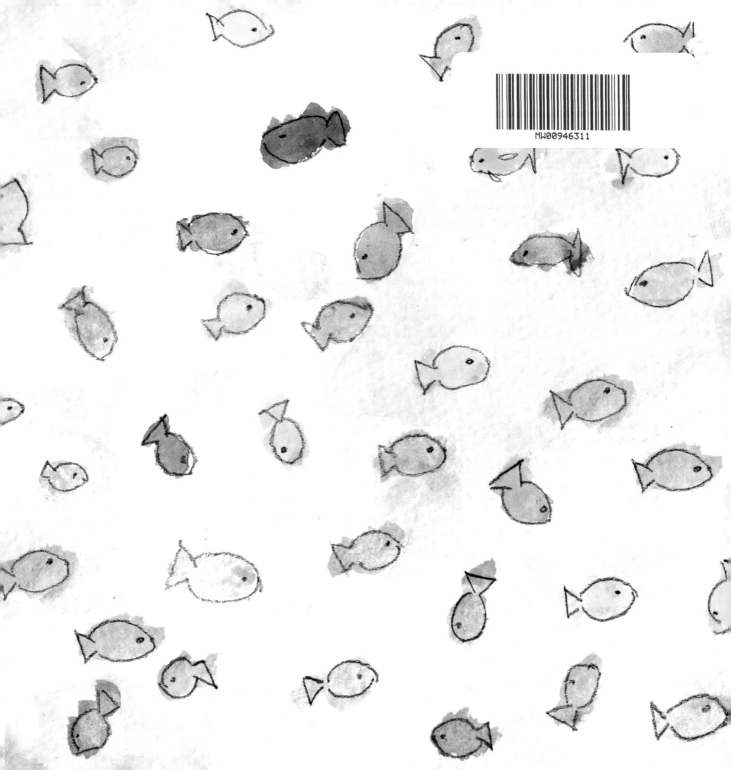

MW00946311

For information please visit
www.booksurge.com
or call
866-308-6235

For more on Sparky please visit
www.GillianLeeHutshing.com

First Edition
ISBN 1-4196-4240-5

Printed in the United States of America

Text and Illustrations
Gillian Lee Hutshing

Art Direction and Design
Serban Cristescu

Legal Guardian
Susan A. Grode

*Special Thanks to
Mili Smythe and
Susan Grode*

*"Sparky" is based
on a true story.*

*The real Sparky
lived happily in his
bowl for 13 years!*

Sparky
the
Wonder
A story of how love creates magic fish

Hi Michelle !!!

Written & Illustrated by Gillian Lee Hutshing

Once there was a little girl named Mary.
Mary had curly red hair and bright blue eyes.
She was a very small girl with a very big heart.

One bright, Summer day Mary's father
poured six large fish into the new giant fish tank that
sat atop the living room table.

As the big ugly fish surveyed their new surroundings,
Mary stepped into the room.

…When she spotted the tank, she gave dad a *yank!*

Pulling him close to the curious creatures,
Mary wondered aloud about their strange features.
"Daddy, what kind of fish are those in that crowd?"
The biggest lounged, leering and LICKING his chops.
Her father replied, "They are called 'OSCARS' and they are
very hungry - Come on honey, we have to get
them some food from the store."

"GGRRARGHH,"

said his stomach as they walked out the door!
BANG!

Inside the pet store Mary was thrilled.

"Oh dad, they're so cute!"
she said, face to the glass, watching the tiny tads
all racing around.

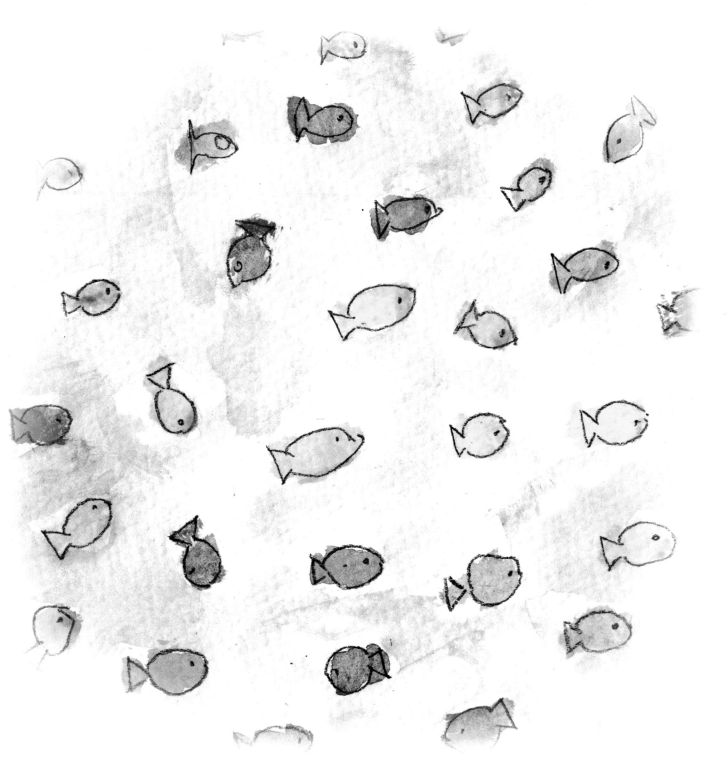

Her father said gently,
"Honey, those are the fish that we came here to buy.
But don't get your hopes up too terribly high…

They FEED the eaters - they're goldfish called, 'FEEDERS'

They'll be EATEN by BIG fish and end up in their TUMMY!
The OSCARS that WE have will find them *quite* YUMMY!"

JUST then, from the thousands of frolicking fellows,
Mary noticed one in particular - fins flapping about.

As she put her hand closer as if to
touch him, he SPED lickety-split up to see her.

He stared right at Mary - straight into her eyes.
She was so pleased, that she cried out with ease, "SPARKY!"

SO that was his name on the spot - *quick as that!*

At precisely this moment her dad grabbed a net.
SWOOOSH into the water it slipped - scooping dozens of
feeders in one single *SWISH!* Sparky'd been MISSED!

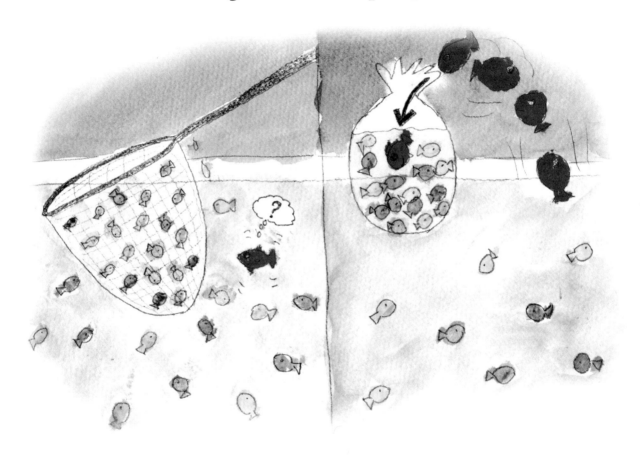

He wanted to come but what could he DO?
He had to think FAST! He FLUNG himself fearlessly
out of the tank, fins over teakettle,
SPLOOOSH into the bag - *just in time!*

Mary looked at her father and
BEAMED!

…This little guy liked her - or so it *seemed!*

As they drove home,
perched on her lap
was the big bag
of feeders swimming
happily about.

ALL of a sudden,
Mary felt the bag
MOVE!

Upon looking
down can you guess
what she SAW?

The very same fish she had seen in the store,
was trying to get her ATTENTION once more…

BONKING his nose *right* into the bag.
"Oh, it's YOU again, *hello*" she said.

At home when the frisky fish were
FREED from the bag…

Sparky tried to hold on with all that he had -
Clinging, then *sliding*…

SPLASH!

…into the water,
Smack-dab in
the midst of those
big-toothed
BEASTS!

Oh NO!
Mary GASPED!

She BEGGED her father to save them from their
AWFUL fate, "Please daddy can't we save them, please?"

But he said, "Don't worry sweetheart, as I told you before,
the big ones eat the little ones - that's what feeders are for."

In spite of his words, Mary was scared for their plight
and scrambled for something to make it all right!

JUST as the BIGGEST was GULPING down fish,
that is when Mary got her very first wish! (*a net*)

As she PLUNGED the net deep into the water, OSCAR was *charging*, BEARING DOWN on the savory swimmers: Slurping FOUR, SIX, *sometimes* TEN at a TIME!!!

CHOMP! CHOMP!! CHOMP!!!

She HAD to save at least *ONE!*
But before she got CLOSE to the jaws of that
MEAT-EATING monster, that CARNIVOROUS cad
he'd whisked even more up!

It was BAD! BAD! **BAD! BAD!**

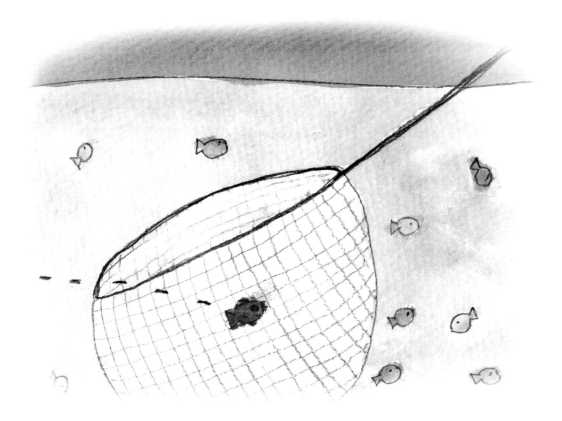

Just THEN, into her net…He swam, the littlest fish,
the teeniest tiniest of the glistening gang.

It was the feeder who'd been friendly BEFORE,
at the store, in the car and now once MORE! *Sparky.*

She SCOOPED him out - *SWOOOSH!*

This fearless fellow flopped and he splashed and he
squirmed in this spot…

He must be CONFUSED - that's what she thought!

Mary ran QUICK to the kitchen for a BIG dish of water,
then RUSHED to her friend and said,
"In you go - just like an OTTER!"

Mary had to get Dad out the door
and BACK to that store!

She thought it wise
to buy Sparky some SUPPLIES.

She chose a BIG round bowl, LOTS of bright blue gravel,
SOME flaky fish food and A nice living plant!

Mary was about to pay
for her things, when the man
at the counter, who was *quite* round indeed,
asked, "May I inquire young lady, for what
kind of fish are the things that you need?"

Mary answered excitedly, "It's for one of your tiniest
goldfish; one I got yesterday here with my father!"

The man looked as though something was wrong
and said, "Sweetie, those are just food for
BIG fish - they aren't very STRONG.

...Not even as strong as a fish you might win at the fair.
And the chance he might live is undoubtedly RARE.
I'm so sorry my dear that I don't have good news,
perhaps there's ANOTHER one that you should choose."

Mary couldn't believe what she heard!

Fighting back TEARS in her eyes…
She left the store WITHOUT her supplies.

As she walked through the front door of her house,
Mary let out a *SQUEAL*…

…And ran to make sure it was REAL!
To her sheer *delight* and utter *surprise*,
there he was, right in front of her eyes!
Her tiny fish *ZOOMING* around and around
and around in the DISH!!!

It was her BIGGEST wish - that her *brave*
little friend, from the store and the car and the dish,
really WAS a strong fish!

The following morning
MARY'S dad woke her with a big GRIN on his face…

And do you KNOW what her father did *next?*

He placed "SPARKY…THE WONDERFISH"
in his *beautiful* new bowl on the white
kitchen table, by the BIG picture window.

The BOWL with the bright *blue* gravel
and the nice *living* plant!

Sparky was STOKED!
He *leaped* in the air with APLOMB!

Then *whizzed* round and round with light
flashing off his sparkling scales!

Thanks to her he was ALIVE
and thanks to her, he now would THRIVE!

And from THEN on…

EVERY time she put her hand to the GLASS as she had
on that very FIRST day, SPARKY would swim to it - looking up
into her eyes, as if to say, "Thank you MARY, I love you TOO!
THAT'S why I *lived* - to BE with *YOU!!!*"

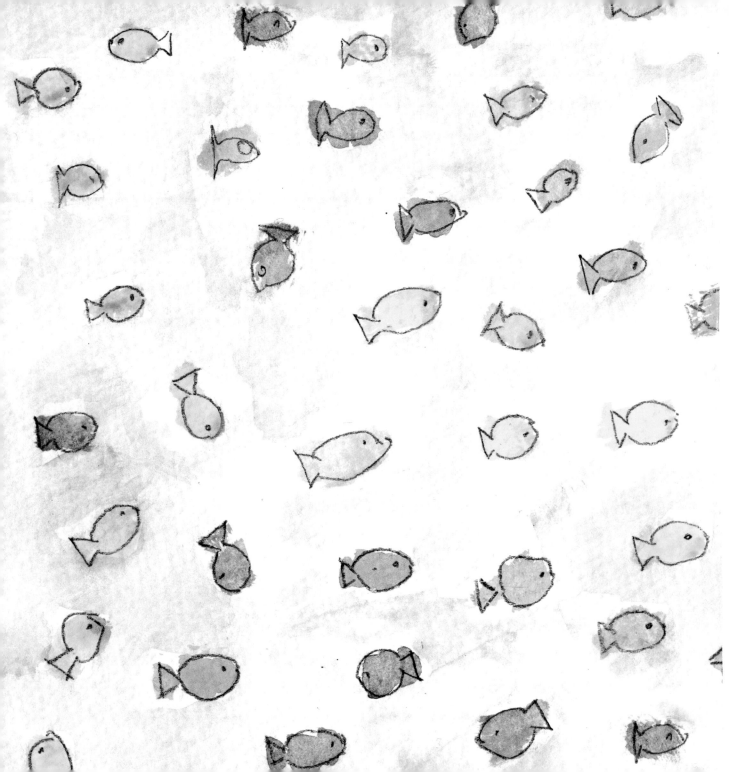